THE BOY WHO NEVER HAD A FRIEND

Charlie B. Bush Jr.

Infusionmedia
2124 Y St #138
Lincoln, NE 68503
https://infusion.media

Printed in the United States
10 9 8 7 6 5 4 3 2 1

First Edition

ISBN: 978-1-945834-25-7

Library of Congress Control Number: 2021912830

Illustrations by Charles Dorse

To my son, Charlie B. Bush III

Once upon a time, there was a boy who never had a friend. He grew up with his two sisters, his mom, and his dad. One sister named Royla was six years old, and the other one, Tinana, was five.

The boy who never had a friend was Charlie III, called Charlie the third. He was named after his father, who was named after his father. Charlie was ten. He never went anywhere because his parents were too poor.

They didn't own a car, and they stayed at home way out in the country. Charlie the third dreamed of being a football player. He always asked his mom and dad if they would sign him up to play sports. His parents would always tell him that it cost money to sign up to play sports.

At night, Charlie the third would look out the window at the stars in the sky. He would look out the window for hours, and all he would do was cry. "I don't have any friends," he would say. "I get tired of playing with my sisters all day. They can't play football. They can't play baseball. They can't play anything. They're just too small."

One day Charlie the third got off the bus from school and saw his mom and dad moving things onto a truck. He yelled, "Mom, Dad, what are you doing?" Dad said, "Charlie the third, we have to move." His mom and dad continued to pack their clothes onto the neighbor's truck. Charlie the third and his family moved into town to live with Uncle Chuck.

Charlie the third wasn't used to city life. When he looked out the window at night, all he saw were big lights. He heard fire trucks and police cars all through the night. He heard firecrackers and people yelling like they were in a fight. He would ask his dad, "What is that noise?" His dad would say, "Charlie the third, those are some bad boys."

Charlie the third would say, "What's bad about popping fire crackers?" but little did he know it was guns they were capping. Charlie the third's dad would always tell him to stay inside. That made him sad, and all he did was cry.

One day he asked his mom, "Why can't I go out-
side?" She said, "Charlie the third, when your
uncle gets back here, he's going to take you
for a long ride." About that time, Uncle Chuck
was pulling up into the drive. Charlie the third
rushed to the door, yelling, "Uncle Chuck, are we
going for a ride?" Uncle Chuck said, "Yes, Charlie
the third, but first I must go inside."

He went inside to change his clothes. When he came back out, he yelled, "Charlie the third, I'm ready to roll." They both got into the car and put on their seat belts. They took a trip uptown, downtown, and all around town. When they came to a park, it was on the other side of town. Charlie the third saw the swings and the football field and yelled, "Uncle Chuck, Uncle Chuck, right here! Right here!"

Uncle Chuck parked his car, and Charlie the third got out. He ran to the swings without a doubt. There he met a group of kids, ages ten through sixteen. He asked one of the kids if he could have a swing. The oldest one said, "You must be on the team." Charlie the third asked, "What does that mean?" The oldest kid said, "We're in a gang. If you want to join us, then you can swing."

Charlie the third didn't know what exactly a gang was, so he said yes so he could have a swing. The oldest boy said, "You must be initiated to be in our gang." Charlie the third said OK just so he could swing. The ten-year-old boy walked up and punched Charlie the third in the eye. Charlie the third fell to his knees and began to cry. Then the thirteen-year-old walked up and kicked him. Charlie the third grabbed his stomach, then hauled off and hit him. Then all the kids jumped Charlie the third and began to stomp him. About that time, Uncle Chuck ran over and said, "What's going on here?"

The oldest boy said, "He wanted to join our gang." Uncle Chuck asked, "For what?" The ten-year-old said, "So he could have a swing." At that point, Charlie the third got off the ground, holding his stomach without making a sound.

He yelled at them all, "I don't want to play your dumb games." The oldest boy said, "You're in now. You can have a swing." Charlie the third said, "No. You can keep your swing because if I have to hurt people, I don't want to be in a gang."

The ten-year-old stood up and said, "He's right. I don't want to be in this dumb gang 'cause all we do is fight." The thirteen-year-old came forward and said, "Me neither. I can have better fun than hurting other people." The sixteen-year-old looked sad and dropped his head. He said, "I was wrong. I'm sorry for what I have done. Can we still be friends and stop this dumb gang?"

Charlie the third said, "Yes, but first I need to know all your names." The sixteen-year-old said, "My name is Sean." The ten-year-old said, "My name is Dee." The thirteen-year-old said, "My name is Lil Johnny." The eleven-year-old said, "My name is Montez." "My name is Charlie the third," said Charlie the third. "I just moved here, and I don't like gangs, but I like to play games."

Dee asked, "What do you play?" Charlie the third said, "I play football, baseball, basketball, and soccer." The other kids told Charlie the third that they were sorry and asked if they could meet at the playground and play tomorrow.

Dee said, "I'll bring my football." Lil Johnny said, "I will bring my basketball." Sean said, "I will bring my soccer ball," and Montez said, "I will bring my baseball." Charlie the third looked at his Uncle Chuck and asked, "Uncle Chuck, could we come tomorrow?" Uncle Chuck said, "Yes, Charlie the third," and they all said they were sorry.

THE END